Mrs Pepperpot's Busy Day

Story by ALF PRØYSEN

Illustrated by BJÖRN BERG

Translated by MARIANNE HELWEG

PUFFIN BOOKS

1

There was once an old woman who went to bed at night as old women usually do, and in the morning she woke up as old women usually do. But on this particular morning she found herself shrunk to the size of a pepperpot, and old women don't usually do that. The odd thing was, her name really was Mrs Pepperpot.

'Well, as I'm now the size of a pepperpot, I shall have to make the best of it,' she said to herself, for she had no one else to talk to; her husband was out in the fields and all her children were grown up and gone away.

Now she happened to have a great deal to do that day. First of all she had to clean the house, then there was all the washing which was waiting to be done, and lastly she had to make pancakes for supper.

'I must get out of bed somehow,' she thought, and, taking hold of a corner of the eiderdown, she pushed it to the side of the bed and started to climb down it. In the end she found herself underneath it on the floor. Mrs Pepperpot crawled out and she hadn't hurt herself a bit.

The first job was to clean the house, but that was quite easy; she just squatted down in front of a mouse-hole and squeaked till the mouse came out.

'Clean the house from top to bottom' she said, 'or I'll tell the cat about you.' So the mouse cleaned the house from top to bottom.

Mrs Pepperpot called the cat: 'Puss! Puss! Lick all the plates and dishes or I'll tell the dog about you.' And the cat licked all the plates and dishes clean.

Then the old woman called the dog. 'Listen, dog; you make the bed and open the window and I'll give you a bone as a reward.' So the dog did as he was told, and when he had finished he sat down on the front doorstep and waved his tail so hard he made the step shine like a mirror.

'You'll have to get the bone yourself,' said Mrs Pepperpot, 'I haven't time to wait on people.' She pointed to the window-sill where a large bone lay.

After this she wanted to start her washing. She had put it to soak in the brook, but the brook was almost dry. So she sat down and started muttering in a cross sort of way:

'I have lived a long time, but in all my born days I never saw the brook so dry. If we don't have a shower soon, I expect everyone will die of thirst.' Over and over again she said it, all the time looking up at the sky.

At last the raincloud in the sky got so angry that it decided to drown the old woman altogether. But she crawled under a monk's-hood flower, where she stayed snug and warm while the rain poured down and rinsed her clothes clean in the brook.

Now the old woman started muttering again: 'I have lived a long time, but in all my born days I have never known such a feeble south wind as we have had lately. I'm sure if the south wind started blowing this minute it couldn't lift me off the ground, even though I am no bigger than a pepperpot.'

The south wind heard this and instantly came tearing along, but Mrs Pepperpot hid in an empty badger set, and from there she watched the south wind blow all the clothes right up on to her clothes-line.

Again she started muttering: 'I have lived a long time, but in all my born days I have never seen the sun give so little heat in the middle of the summer. It seems to have lost all its power, that's a fact.'

When the sun heard this it turned scarlet with rage and sent down fiery rays to give the old woman sunstroke.

But by this time she was safely back in her house, and was sailing about the sink in a saucer. Meanwhile the furious sun dried all the clothes on the line.

'Now for cooking the supper.' said Mrs Pepperpot; 'my husband will be back in an hour and, by hook or by crook, thirty pancakes must be ready on the table.'

She had mixed the batter for the pancakes the day before, and she had to climb up by a chair to reach the jug containing the batter.

Now she stood before the jug and said: 'I have always been fond of you, jug, and I've told all the neighbours that there's not a jug like you anywhere. I am sure, if you really wanted to, you could walk straight over to the cooking-stove and turn it on.'

And the jug went straight over
to the stove and turned it on.

Then Mrs Pepperpot said: 'I'll never forget the day I bought my frying-pan. There were lots of pans in the shop, but I said: "If I can't have that pan hanging right over the shop assistant's head, I won't buy any pan at all. For that is the best pan in the whole world, and I'm sure if I were ever in trouble that pan could jump on to the stove by itself." '

And there and then the frying-pan jumped on to the stove. And when it was hot enough, the jug tilted itself to let the batter run into the pan.

Then the old woman said: 'I once read a fairy-tale about a pancake which could roll along the road. It was the stupidest story that ever I read. But I'm sure the pancake in the pan could easily turn a somersault in the air if it really wanted to.'

At this the pancake took a great leap from sheer pride and turned a somersault as Mrs Pepperpot had said. Not only one pancake, but *all* the pancakes did this, and the jug went on tilting and the pan went on frying until, before the hour was up, there were thirty pancakes on the dish.

Then Mr Pepperpot came home. And, just as he opened the door, Mrs Pepperpot turned back to her usual size. So they sat down and ate their supper.

And the old woman said nothing about having been as small as a pepperpot, because old women don't usually talk about such things.